NONYE AND A PRECIOUS JEWELRY

Story of a desirous charming lady and her necklace journey

By Annie Miriam

Table of Contents

Introduction:

A complete story of an unfortunate but fortunate young beautiful lady who crave for good things of life though nothing comes in a platter of gold. This made her took some decisions and actions that affected her. It is amazing how the whole thing became a reality but life keeps staging her to become what she is. The end is unimaginable and a lesson to learn.

Chapter 1

Nonye and her Hearth Desires

She was one of those attractive and charming ladies born, as if by a mistake of destiny, into a family of clerks. She had no dowry, no aspirations, no means of being recognized, understood, loved, or wedded by a man of money and reputation; and so she let herself get married to a junior official at the Ministry of Education. She dressed casually because she had never been able to buy anything more, yet she was as sad as if she had previously been affluent. Women don't belong to a caste or class; their beauty, elegance, and natural appeal take the place of birth and family. Natural delicacy, innate grace, and quick wit set their standing in society, and make the daughters of commoners the equals of the very greatest women. She suffered ceaselessly, believing she was entitled to enjoy the delights and luxuries of life. She agonized because of the poorness of her home as she glanced at the unclean walls, the worn-out furniture, and the unsightly drapes. All these things that another lady of her status would not even have noticed, plagued her and made her bitter. The sight of the small Brenton girl who did her chores filled her with dreadful emotions and forlorn desires. She dreamt of hushed antechambers draped with Oriental tapestries, lighted from above by torches in bronze holders, while two tall footmen in knee-length breeches rested in big armchairs, weary from the stove's suffocating warmth. She dreamt of enormous living rooms dressed in rare ancient silks, magnificent furniture laden with expensive decorations, and pleasant smaller chambers, scented, intended for afternoon discussions with intimate friends - renowned, sought-after men, who all women envy and want. When she sat down to dine at a circular table covered with a three-day-old cloth opposite her husband who, pulling the top off the soup, screamed joyfully, "Ah! Beef stew! What could be better," she dreamed of fine dinners, of shining silverware, of tapestries which peopled the walls with figures from another time and strange birds in fairy forests; she dreamed of delicious dishes served on wonderful plates, of whispered gallantries listened to with an inscrutable smile as one ate the pink flesh of a trout or the wings of a quail.

She had no gowns, no jewelry, nothing; yet these were the only things she loved. She believed she was designed for them alone. She wanted so much to captivate, to be envied, to be desired and sought after. She had a wealthy acquaintance, a former schoolmate at the convent, whom she no longer wanted to see since she suffered so much when she returned home. For full days following she would cry with grief, regret, despair, and misery.\s*

One evening her husband arrived home with an expression of victory, clutching a huge package in his hand.

"Look," he continued, "here's something for you."

She tore open the paper and brought out a card, on which was written the words:\s

"The Minister of Education and Mme. Georges Rampouneau seeks the pleasure of M. and Mme. Nonye's company at the Ministry, on the evening of Monday, January 18th."

Instead of being happy, as her husband had planned, she flung the invitation on the table resentfully, and muttered:\s "What do you expect me to do with that?" "But, my darling, I thought you would be happy. You seldom go out, and it will be such a nice event! I had tremendous problems acquiring it. Everyone wants to attend; it is quite exclusive, and they're not providing many invites to clerks. The entire ministry will be there." She glanced at him fiercely, and asked, impatiently:\s "And what do you want me to wear if I go?" He hadn't thought about it. He stammered:\s "Why the outfit you go to the theatre in? It feels really lovely to me ..." He halted, surprised, horrified to find his wife sobbing. Two huge tears trickled slowly from the corners of her eyes towards the corners of her lips. He stuttered:\s "What's the matter? What's the matter?" With a tremendous effort, she controlled her anguish and responded in a calm voice, as she dried her tearful cheeks:\s "Nothing. Only I have no dress and thus I can't attend this party. Give your invitation to a buddy whose wife has finer clothing than I do." He was unhappy, but tried again:\s "see, Let's, Stephanie. How much would a decent dress cost, one which you could wear again on other occasions, something really simple?" She considered for a time, figuring the cost, and also thinking about what much she could ask for without an abrupt denial and a frightened cry from the frugal cashier. At last, she said hesitantly:\s "I don't know precisely, but I suppose I could accomplish it with four hundred dollars." He became a bit pink, for he had been saving that precise amount to purchase a rifle and treat himself to a hunting trip the next summer, in the area outside Nanterre, with a few acquaintances who went lark-shooting there on Sundays. However, he said:\s "Very right, I can offer you four hundred dollars. But try to find a very stunning garment."

*

The day of the celebration came nigh, and Madame Nonye appeared melancholy, restless, apprehensive. Her clothing was ready, though. One evening her spouse inquired to her:\s "the What's matter? You've been behaving peculiarly these past three days." She replied: "I'm unhappy because I have no diamonds, not a single stone to wear. It will appear cheap. I would almost prefer not to attend the party." "You may wear flowers, " he continued, "They are stylish at this time of year. For ten dollars you might obtain two or three gorgeous roses." She was not persuaded. "No; there is nothing more embarrassing than appearing impoverished in the presence of a bunch of affluent ladies." "How dumb you are!" her husband shouted. "Go and visit your acquaintance Madame Johanna and ask her to give you some diamonds. You know her well enough for that." She gave a yell of pleasure. "Of course. I had not thought about it." The following day she went to her friend's home and informed her of her difficulties. Madame Johanna walked to her mirrored closet, pulled out a huge box, brought it back, opened it, and said to Madame Nonye:\s "Choose, my darling." First, she noticed various bracelets, then a pearl necklace, then a gold Venetian cross adorned with magnificent stones, of excellent workmanship. She tried on the jewels in the mirror, hesitated, could not bear to part with them, to give them back. She continued asking:\s "You have nothing else?"

"Why, yeah. But I don't know what you enjoy." Suddenly she found, in a black satin box, a spectacular diamond necklace, and her heart started to beat with unrestrained passion. Her hands shook as she grasped it. She wrapped it around her neck, over her high-necked dress, and stood lost in bliss as she stared at herself. Then she said hesitantly, hesitating:\s "Why, yeah, of course." She wrapped her arms around her friend's neck, hugged her rapturously, and departed with her treasure.\s*
The day of the celebration came. Madame Nonye was a success. She was more beautiful than all the other ladies, stylish, charming, smiling and full of delight. All the males gazed at her, asked her name, and attempted to be acquainted. All the cabinet officials wanted to waltz with her. The minister spotted her.

Chapter 2

The Party and After Party

She danced wildly, with passion, drunk on pleasure, forgetting everything in the triumph of her beauty, in the glory of her success, in a sort of cloud of happiness, made up of all this respect, all this admiration, all these awakened desires, of that sense of triumph that is so sweet to a woman's heart.

She departed at approximately four o'clock in the morning. Her husband had been asleep since midnight in a tiny vacant anteroom with three other gentlemen whose wives were having a fine time. He put over her shoulders the clothing he had prepared for her to walk outside in, the simple garments of everyday existence, whose poverty contrasted strongly with the luxury of the ball dress. She sensed this and wanted to flee away, so she wouldn't be spotted by the other ladies who were enveloping themselves in costly furs. Nonye held her back. "Wait a bit, you'll get a cold outdoors. I'll go and locate a taxi." But she did not listen to him and hurried down the stairs. When they were finally on the street, they could not locate a taxi and started to hunt for one, calling at the cabmen they saw passing in the distance.

They headed down toward the Seine in despair, shivering with cold. At last, they located on the quay one of those ancient night taxis that one sees in Paris only after dark, as if they were afraid to reveal their shabbiness during the day. They were left off at their door in the Rue des

Martyrs and regretfully went up the stairs to their flat. It was all over, for her. And he was recalling that he had to be back at his workplace at 10 o'clock. In front of the mirror, she peeled off the clothing over her shoulders, taking a last look at herself in all her beauty. But immediately she emitted a shriek. She no longer had the jewelry encircling her neck! "What is the matter?" inquired her husband, already half naked. She turned towards him, panic-stricken. "I have ... I have ... I no longer have Madame Johanna 's jewelry." He stood up, disturbed. "What! ... how! ... That's impossible!" They searched in the folds of her garment, in the folds of her cloak, in her pockets, everywhere. But they could not discover it. "Are you sure you still had it on when you left the ball?" he inquired. "Yes. I touched it in the hall at the Ministry." "But if you had lost it on the street we would have heard it fall. It must be in the cab." "Yes. That's probably it. Did you take his number?" "No. And you, didn't you see it?" "No." They gazed at one other, shocked. At last, Nonye put his clothes on again. "I'm going back," he replied, "over the full path we went, see if I can locate it."

He departed. She stayed in her ball dress all evening, without the strength to go to bed, sitting on a chair, with no fire, her thoughts blank. Her spouse returned at approximately seven o'clock. He had discovered nothing. He went to the police, to the press to offer a reward, to the taxi companies, anywhere the faintest flicker of hope led him. She waited all day, in the same mood of blank hopelessness as before this awful event. Nonye returned in the evening, a hollow, colorless figure; he had discovered nothing. "You must write to your friend,"

he urged, "inform her you have broken the clasp of her necklace and that you are having it fixed. It will give us time to search some more."
She wrote as he dictated.\s*
At the end of one week, they had lost all hope.
And Nonye, who had aged five years, declared:\s "We must decide how to replace the jewel."\s The following day they collected the box which contained it and went to the jeweler whose name they discovered inside. He consulted his books. "It was not I, madame, who sold the jewelry; I must just have provided the container." And so they traveled from jeweler to jeweler, hunting for a necklace like the other one, checking their memories, both ill with sadness and misery. In a boutique in the Palais Royal, they spotted a string of diamonds that looked to be just what they were looking

for. It was worth forty thousand dollars. They may have it for thirty-six thousand. So they asked the jeweler not to sell it for three days. And they struck an understanding that he would take it back for thirty-four thousand dollars if the second necklace was located by the end of February.

Nonye had eighteen thousand dollars that his father had given him. He would borrow the remainder. And he did borrow, asking for a thousand dollars from one guy, five hundred from another, five Louis here, three Louis there. He provided notes, negotiated fatal deals, dealt with usurers, with every sort of money-lender. He compromised the rest of his life, risked signing notes without knowing if he could ever honor them, and, terrified by the anguish still to come, by the black misery about to fall on him, by the prospect of every physical privation and every moral torture he was about to suffer, he went to get the new necklace and laid down on the jeweler's counter thirty-six thousand dollars. When Madame Nonye brought the jewelry back, Madame Johanna stated coldly:\s "You should have returned it sooner, I could have needed it." To the relief of her buddy, she did not open the case. If she had spotted the substitution, what would she have thought? What would she have said? Would she have taken her friend for a thief?\s*

From then on, Madame Nonye learned about the dreadful lives of the extremely poor. But she did her role magnificently. The horrible debt must be paid. She would pay for it. They dismissed their maid; they shifted their accommodations; they hired a garret beneath the roof. She got to know the hardship of housekeeping, and the loathsome labors of the kitchen. She scrubbed the dishes, smearing her rose nails on greasy pots and the bottoms of pans. She washed the filthy linen, the shirts, and the dishcloths, which she strung to dry on a line; she brought the rubbish down to the street every morning, and carried up the water, halting at each landing to collect her breath. And, dressed like a commoner, she walked to the fruiterer's, the grocer's, the butcher's, her basket on her arm, negotiating, offended, fighting over every miserable sou.

Each month they had to pay some notes, renew others, and gain additional time.

Her husband worked every evening, writing accounting for a shopkeeper, and frequently, late into the night, he sat transcribing a manuscript at five sous a page.

And this existence lasted 10 years.

At the end of 10 years, they had paid off everything, everything, at usurer's rates and with the accumulations of compound interest.

Madame Nonye looked ancient now. She had grown powerful, harsh, and brutal like other women of destitute houses. With hair half combed, with skirts awry, and reddened hands, she talked loudly as she washed the floor with great swishes of water. But occasionally, while her husband was at the office, she sat down near the window and thought about that evening at the ball so long ago, when she had been so lovely and so appreciated. What would have occurred if she had not lost the necklace? Who knows, who knows? How odd life is, how fickle! How little is required for one to be wrecked or rescued!

One Sunday, when she was strolling through the Champs Élysées to refresh herself after the week's job, unexpectedly she observed a mother walking with a kid. It was Madame Johanna , still young, still lovely, still charming. Madame Nonye felt emotional. Should she talk to her? Yes, of course. And now that she had paid, she would tell her everything. Why not? She walked up to her. "Good morning, Jeanne." The other, shocked to be treated so familiarly by this plain lady, could not identify her. She stammered:\s "But - madame - I don't know. You must have made a mistake." "No, I am Stephanie Nonye." Her companion shouted a scream. "Oh! ... my poor Stephanie, how you've changed! ..." "Yes, I have had some hard times since I last saw you, and many sorrows ... and all because of you! ..." "Me? How can it be?" "You recall that diamond necklace that you loaned me to wear to the Ministry party?" "Yes. Well?" "Well, I lost it." "What do you mean? You brought it back." "I brought you back another just like it. And it has taken us 10 years to pay for it. It wasn't easy for us, we had very little. But at last, everything is finished, and I am quite pleased." Madame Johanna was astonished. "You claim that you purchased a diamond necklace to replace mine?" "Yes; you didn't notice then? They were pretty similar." And she grinned with proud and naive joy. Madame Johanna , greatly affected, grasped both her hands.

"Oh, my poor Stephanie! Mine was an imitation! It was worth five hundred dollars at most! ..." So she took her back to her home and opened the box where the diamond neckless was and wore it on Madame Nonye and said to her "this will be on good fitting for you" with a smile and joy, Nonye replied calmly "yes" then

Madame Johanna gave it out as a gift for being truthful and open to truth.

Madame Nonye went home happy and jubilating for she has found favor and joy of her life, then she explained to her husband about her movement and showed him the neckless, they hugged each other and celebrated. It was the best night ever for the love birds.

The next day, they took the neckless back to the jeweler to be sold and jeweler happily bought them and even paid her more than what she bought them. They went home with the money and made merry together. This was a nice time for the couple.

www.ingramcontent.com/pod-product-compliance
Lightning Source LLC
LaVergne TN
LVHW020547160826
845677LV00015B/4244
* 9 7 9 8 8 4 7 5 1 4 0 5 7 *